I'm Your Peanut Butter BIG BROTHER

Selina Alko

Alfred A. Knopf ❧ New York

To Isaiah and Ginger

Baby brother
or sister,
will you look
like me?

I blend from semisweet dark Daddy chocolate bar **and** strawberry cream Mama's milk.

Starry night sky and lemon meringue sunshine,

Daddy and Mommy

blend a mocha cloud.

Ginger cookie brown or midnight licorice purple?

When we play,

will you, like Lola, leap,
cappuccino-frosted 'fro
bouncing along?

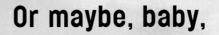

Or maybe, baby,

you will wind down the slide

just like pecan
elastic band Sebastian.

At the beach,

will you stretch high, building tall caramel towers with Uncle Mike?

Or

like Cousin Chloe, will you dig deep in pumpkin puddles below?

Cinnamon sand castle
baby-to-be.

Will you be my vanilla bean ice cream sibling

or

super-rich double chocolate fudge?

Baby, will your hair look like mine?

Akira's puffy head of broccoli flowerets?

Noel's string beans locked this way and that

or

Maybe, like Aunty Angela, your mushroom bob will wave neatly in half-moon curls.

Or, like Grandma Helen, will sharp blades of grass stick straight up?

Feathers might hang from a round coconut face.

Sister- or brother-to-be, will your eyes have my shape?

**Hot cocoa footballs
set wide apart**

or

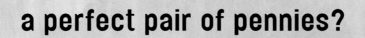

a perfect pair of pennies?

My eyes blend from
Daddy's charcoal tires

and

Mama's honey-roasted almonds.

What color
will your
eyes be?

**Baby,
will your
lips shape
like mine?**

My soft rose petals smack sugar on
Mommy's jelly-bean smile.

our room,

walls ocean violet and chalkboard black.

Pirates' golden crib

and bouncy fire-
engine seat.

Ready, set, go!
All painted fresh for you.

Brother- or Sister-to-be,

together we will dream, draw, wrestle and play,
do projects, sing, snack, chill, read and sleep.

Baby sister!

Here at last with me.

THIS IS A BORZOI BOOK PUBLISHED BY ALFRED A. KNOPF

Copyright © 2009 by Selina Alko

All rights reserved. Published in the United States by Alfred A. Knopf, an imprint of Random House Children's Books, a division of Random House, Inc., New York.

Knopf, Borzoi Books, and the colophon are registered trademarks of Random House, Inc.

Visit us on the Web! www.randomhouse.com/kids

Educators and librarians, for a variety of teaching tools, visit us at www.randomhouse.com/teachers

Library of Congress Cataloging-in-Publication Data
Alko, Selina.
I'm your peanut butter big brother / Selina Alko. — 1st ed.
p.   cm.
Summary: A child in an interracial family wonders what his yet-to-be-born sibling will look like.
ISBN 978-0-375-85627-3 (trade) — ISBN 978-0-375-95627-0 (lib. bdg.)
[1. Racially mixed people—Fiction. 2. Babies—Fiction. 3. Brothers and sisters—Fiction.] I. Title.
PZ7.A39843 lm 2009   [E]—dc22   2008010345

The illustrations in this book were created using gouache and mixed media.

MANUFACTURED IN MALAYSIA
March 2009
10 9 8 7 6 5 4 3 2 1

First Edition

Acknowledgments

I'd like to acknowledge Emily Bibby, our next-door neighbor, whose childlike curiosity sparked the original idea for my book. My appreciation also goes to Monica Wellington, whose children's book writing and illustrating class I was enrolled in when I developed this story. Many thanks to Rebecca Sherman, my excellent agent, for helping me rework the story to make it both more personal and more poetic. I give special thanks to my editor, Erin Clarke, for taking a chance with my first book as both author and illustrator. And to Melissa Nelson for her awesome art direction. I thank them both for their infectious enthusiasm (and great lunches!). I also want to mention my younger sister, Karen, and our unique sibling relationship, which influenced my writing of this book as well. My infinite gratitude goes to my husband, Sean Qualls, for his constant support, feedback and love. Without him this book would literally have no "father." Our children, Isaiah and Ginger, are the best! I thank them most of all for bringing such immense joy and inspiration into our lives.